For Super Gran. You're the best!
With all my love, Em xxx

Bloomsbury Publishing, London, Oxford, New York, New Delhi and Sydney

First published in Great Britain in 2017 by Bloomsbury Publishing Plc
50 Bedford Square, London WC1B 3DP

www.bloomsbury.com

BLOOMSBURY is a registered trademark of Bloomsbury Publishing Plc

Text and illustrations copyright © Emily MacKenzie 2017
The moral rights of the author/illustrator have been asserted

A CIP catalogue record of this book is available from the British Library

ISBN 978 1 4088 7329 8 (HB)
ISBN 978 1 4088 7330 4 (PB)
ISBN 978 1 4088 7328 1 (eBook)

All papers used by Bloomsbury Publishing are natural, recyclable products made
from wood grown in well managed forests. The manufacturing processes
conform to the environmental regulations of the country of origin

Printed in China by Leo Paper Products, Heshan, Guangdong

1 3 5 7 9 10 8 6 4 2

There's BROCCOLI in my ICE CREAM!

Emily MacKenzie

BLOOMSBURY

LONDON OXFORD NEW YORK NEW DELHI SYDNEY

There was **NOTHING** good about fruit and vegetables in Granville's opinion.

Why on earth would **anyone** want to eat
green things that **crunched**, yellow things that **mushed**
and red things that **squashed**...

especially when there were so many **sweet sugary cakey** things,
cold creamy slurpy things
and **chocky wocky gooey** things to eat instead?

"But Granville," said Mum,
"vegetables are SO good for you!"

"You'll grow up to be big and strong –
just like me!" said Dad.

"Look, Dino LOVES crunchy apples,"
added his sister, Poppy.

"You won't be able to see in the dark
if you don't eat your carrots!"
warned Uncle Bob.

But Granville **didn't** care.
He felt big and strong already,
and if Dino wanted to eat apples,
that was fine by him.

The trouble was that no one in Granville's family gave up that easily.

Granville KNEW that hidden on his plate of things he DID like,
he would ALWAYS find a vegetable lurking somewhere...

Crowned Carrot contest Champion

Most Marvellous Mushrooms Medal

King of the Cauliflowers

Winner of the Prettiest Pumpkin Prize (Two years running!)

Being the youngest in a very long line of greengrocers and prize-winning gardeners, Granville's hatred of all things green and juicy was, well, rather disappointing...

Legendary Leek Grower

Winner of the Colossal Cabbage Cup

...Especially for his Grandpa Reggie –
proud owner of Reggie's Veggies Van.

He was **passionate** about **parsnips**,
mad about **mushrooms**
and absolutely **bonkers** about **broccoli**.

He had even won an award for his marvellous fruit and vegetables –

THE MAGNIFICENT
MAGIC WATERING CAN.

It made everything he planted grow even
faster and taste EVEN MORE DELICIOUS!

So, you see, Granville's hatred of broccoli and beans,
peaches and pears, cabbages and courgettes just wouldn't do.
One night, while Granville was fast asleep,
his family gathered in Grandpa Reggie's
potting shed for a TOP SECRET meeting
and hatched a plan.

The next morning,
they put their **plan** into action.

"Grandpa Reggie," said Poppy innocently,
"what would you like for your birthday?"

"A **pair** of socks?"
suggested Dad.

"How about a new
toothbrush?" said Mum.

"Or a **jigsaw** perhaps?"
said Uncle Bob.

Poor Grandpa, thought Granville. Those presents sound SO boring.

"Grandpa, tell me what you'd REALLY like and
I'll make sure you get it!" he whispered.

The plan was working!

"Well, Granville, funny you should ask!" said Grandpa Reggie.
"What I'd really love for my birthday is for
YOU to grow something we can eat TOGETHER.
I can even let you borrow my MAGNIFICENT MAGIC WATERING CAN."

"OK!" said Granville, surprising everybody.

That afternoon Grandpa Reggie took Granville to the veggie patch to show him what to do.

They weeded ...

raked ...

dug holes ...

planted seeds…

watered the seedlings…

and picked the crops.

At the end of the day they had a **HUGE** basket of fruits and vegetables to sell from Reggie's Veggies Van.

The next morning, Granville arrived at the veggie patch bright and early.
He couldn't wait to get started on a plan of his very own.

Surely, he thought, licking his lips,
if Grandpa's watering can
is REALLY magic, then ANYTHING
I plant will grow to be BIG and DELICIOUS.

ZZZZZ

SOW
AND
GROW

So Granville sowed
pizza slices and burgers,

sweets and
chocolate bars,

cream cakes and biscuits,

and LOTS and LOTS of ice cream and jelly!

Grandpa Reggie was going to LOVE his special birthday garden,
Granville was sure of it!

At last it was
Grandpa's birthday!

Grandpa wanted to open his presents at the veggie patch,
so everybody followed him there . . .

...where they found Granville and the most extraordinary garden!

Nobody had ever seen a jelly jungle or a **pizza plant** before, let alone an absolutely enormous **knickerbocker glory tree**!

"TA DA! HAPPY BIRTHDAY, GRANDPA!" shouted Granville.

"Come and have a taste, Grandpa!
It's DELICIOUS!"

Oh dear. The family plan had failed – most spectacularly!
It was time to try something drastic.

"URGH! BLURGH! YUCK!" said Grandpa Reggie, winking at the others.

Granville was VERY disappointed indeed that Grandpa Reggie didn't like his present.
"The only way you'll get me to try any of that YUCKY ice cream
is if YOU try eating some of this tasty broccoli I grew for YOU!"

Granville went quiet.
Well, maybe he could have just a little tiny taste
to make Grandpa happy on his birthday.

So he bravely opened his mouth, closed his eyes,
nibbled, chewed and gulped.

Granville's family waited nervously for the verdict until he surprised them all.

"Actually, Grandpa, broccoli...isn't too bad!" he declared.
"In fact...it's really rather yummy!"

"Hooray! Yippee! Woohoo!"

Everybody celebrated Grandpa Reggie's birthday
and Granville's broccoli bravery long into the night,
with the most wonderful ice cream and broccoli banquet.

From that day forward **Granville LOVED broccoli!**
He even tried lots of other juicy fruits and crunchy vegetables, too.
Grandpa Reggie was so proud of him that Granville was allowed
to use his Magnificent Magic Watering Can whenever he wanted.

And just like Grandpa Reggie, Granville's
customers loved the things that he grew!